Be Brown!

For Tory Kaletsky and Harley Foos—B.B.

To Rose—B.G.

Reinforced binding suitable for library use

Text copyright © 2002 by Barbara Bottner. Illustrations copyright © 2002 by Barry Gott.
All rights reserved. Book design by Victoria M. Wortmann. Published by The Putnam & Grosset
Group, a division of Penguin Putnam Books for Young Readers, New York. PUTNAM & GROSSET
is a trademark of Penguin Putnam, Inc. Published simultaneously in Canada. Printed in Hong Kong.

Library of Congress Cataloging-in-Publication data is available.

ISBN 0-399-23775-5   A B C D E F G H I J

Be Brown!

by Barbara Bottner   illustrated by Barry Gott

Putnam & Grosset · New York

Stay!

Down!

Come!

Fetch!

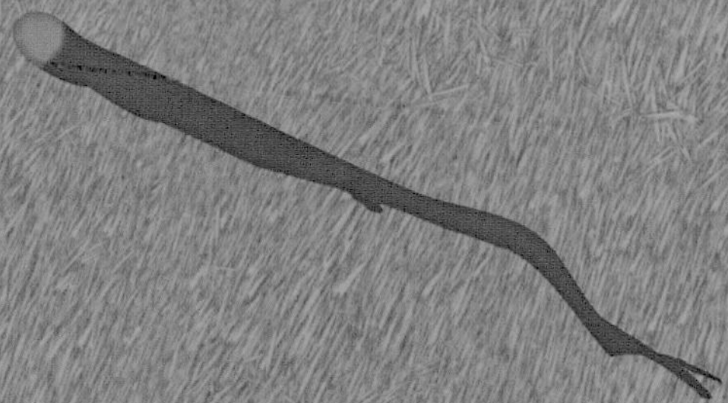

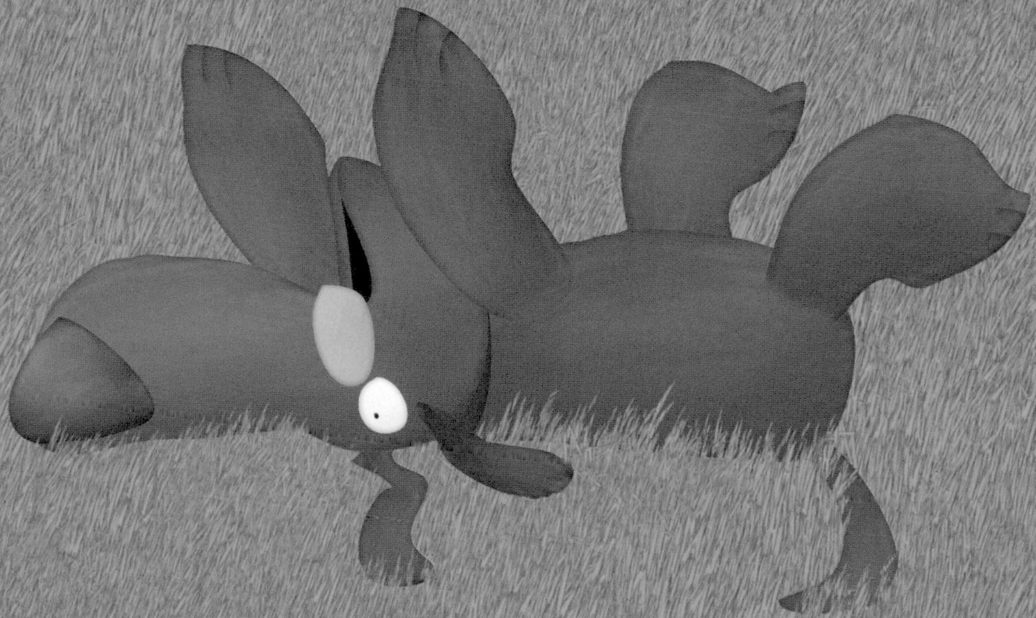

Paw!

Catch!

Drop it!

Be careful!

BE BROWNI

Good dog.